THE GIFT

Joan Lowery Nixon

THE GIFT

Drawings by Andrew Glass

Macmillan Publishing Company
New York

Macmillan Publishing Company
866 Third Avenue, New York, N.Y. 10022
Collier Macmillan Canada, Inc.
Printed in the United States of America

10   9   8   7   6   5   4   3   2

LIBRARY OF CONGRESS CATALOGING IN PUBLICATION DATA
Nixon, Joan Lowery.
  The gift.
  SUMMARY: Brian, visiting his Irish relatives for
the first time, tries to prove to his skeptical
great-aunt that his great-grandfather's tales of
Irish lore and leprechauns are true.
  [1. Ireland—Fiction.   2. Grandfathers—Fiction.
3. Storytelling—Fiction.   4. Leprechauns—Fiction]
I. Glass, Andrew, ill.   II. Title.
PZ7.N65Gi   1983   [Fic]   82-17994
ISBN 0-02-768160-2

For Brian Edward
and
Brian James

with my love

THE GIFT

CHAPTER ONE

Brian didn't know whether to feel more sorry for Grandad or himself. He rubbed at the foggy nose print he had made on the window as he had stared out at the rain, and turned toward his great-grandfather.

"Those are silly tales you've been telling the boy," Aunt Nora said. "His father and mother will think the lot of us are foolish." She lifted the lid from the steaming pot at the back of the huge iron stove, poking under the bubbles with a long wooden spoon.

Aunt Nora reminded Brian of someone, but he couldn't think of who it was. He didn't know if he liked his father's aunt Nora or not. He wished he were back in the United States instead of staying with these Irish relatives he'd never met before, while his parents were at those meetings in Dublin. He wouldn't see his mother and father for at least six weeks—maybe longer. Summer was supposed to be a time for baseball and swimming and friends, but here he was away from home, living on a farm with three old people who probably never saw a baseball game in their whole lives.

His great-grandfather's face crinkled into a grin, but some of the laughter had gone from his blue eyes. "Ah, Nora, there's no harm in my telling Brian about the little people," he said. "The harm is yours for not believing in them."

Grandad looked like one of the little people himself as he hunched on his wooden kitchen chair. His white hair rose in pointy wisps, and his round cheeks were red from the warmth of the room. When he told stories his words rolled out as though they had once been songs.

Brian smiled back at Grandad. "Aunt Nora," he said, "I like to hear Grandad's stories."

"Just remember they're only stories," she said. "And be sure to tell your father that." She moved to the table and put out heavy white plates and bowls and round spoons.

The milky smell of potatoes and onions was making Brian hungry. He was glad it was almost suppertime.

"When Nora was but a girl," Grandad said, "we'd go of an evening with other folk to hear the storyteller. The stories were told so fine that your heart would pound from the wonder of them. I didn't hear Nora saying then that she didn't believe."

"Those stories scared the very life out of me," Aunt

Nora said. "And you, too. They scared everybody! Afterward, we'd walk home down the road in the dark, expecting something to be behind every bush."

"Which there probably was," Grandad said.

Brian laughed, and Aunt Nora turned to him. "Brian doesn't believe your stories," she said. "He's eleven years old—more than halfway to becoming a man—and much too smart for all that nonsense."

They both studied him. Aunt Nora, sure of herself, looked starched all the way to the top of her gray head. Grandad seemed even smaller than he was a few minutes ago.

Now Brian realized who his aunt Nora reminded him of—his best friend, Charlie. Charlie was always sure he knew everything. All that Brian had ever seen or done, Charlie had seen or done first. It was kind of hard to have Charlie for a best friend, but there were a lot of good things about Charlie that made up for it. Brian supposed there must be good things about Aunt Nora, too.

They looked as though they were waiting for his response. The lines around Aunt Nora's mouth had settled into a secure, turned-up pattern as she listened for his words of agreement. Grandad's head was tilted like a bird's, his eyes bright and hopeful. Brian kept himself from smiling at Grandad as he answered. "Mom says scientists always keep open minds. I guess that goes for everyone."

3

Grandad looked so pleased that Brian went on. "There are lots of things we don't have answers for. My friend Charlie's always bragging that he saw a UFO, and he says that once he even lived in a house with a ghost in it."

He thought about the sack of chocolate pieces wrapped to look like gold coins that Charlie had given him as a goodbye present, and which Brian had stuffed in a corner of his suitcase. "Because *you* never had a chance to meet a pirate," Charlie had said. It was the self-important way he said it that made Brian clench his teeth. Brian didn't believe for a minute that Charlie had met a real pirate, as he claimed. And he wasn't too sure about the UFO and the ghost, but Charlie insisted these things had happened, and Brian couldn't prove they hadn't.

Aunt Nora wasn't impressed. "Ghosts! UFO's!" she muttered, rolling her eyes heavenward. She went back to the soup pot, stabbing at the potatoes. "It would be much better," she snapped at the potatoes, "to tell the boy some good, solid Irish history instead."

Grandad's weathered face wrinkled into a smile again, making him look like an apple that had been left too long in the sun. "So it's history you want? It's history you'll get. Pull up a chair, Brian, and I'll tell you some good, solid Irish history."

Brian rested his elbows on the table and his chin in his hands. He wasn't sure he wanted to hear any history. It seemed too much like school. He wished his uncle Martin would finish his farm chores, so they could all sit around the table and eat that soup.

Grandad leaned toward him. "Long ago, in the days when the land was thick with pine forests and great woods of oak and elm, and the mountains were taller and the mists were like heavy cobwebs spread over the valleys, the little people were not so little. They were giants, stretching tall to the sky, and they were magic. They took the land away from the evil folk who lived here. But soon afterward the sons of Mil, who were mortal, came to these shores; and there was a great battle."

"Did the mortals win?" Brian asked.

The lid of the pot came down with a clatter as Grandad said, "Yes, but they struck a bargain with the magic people. The mortals would live on the surface of the earth, and the others in the secret passages and caves under the earth. But those in this in-between world would keep their magic, so the mortals have to be very careful to cooperate with them."

"You said they were giants," Brian interrupted. "How did they get to be little?"

Grandad rubbed the top of his head and stretched. "Oh, there were a couple of reasons. For one, I'm sure that living under the earth interfered with their growth. And sad to say, as fewer and fewer people believed in them, they grew smaller in size."

5

"If there were little people out there I'd surely have seen them," Aunt Nora said. "And all my life I never have. Never!"

"It doesn't surprise me you've never seen one, Nora, with your mind closed as tight as a latched door," Grandad answered. "It's a good thing for you I've got a fine working relationship with the little people, or we'd be in for a lot of mischief from them."

"What kind of mischief?" Brian asked.

Grandad looked to both sides, then leaned forward. In a low voice he said, "They've been known to cause crops to fail, butter to spoil, and cows to stop giving milk."

"Only you would think it was the little people to blame and not the weather," Aunt Nora sniffed.

"What has the weather to do with spoiled butter?" Grandad asked. He turned back to Brian. "When I was but a boy, Molly Ryan over in Mayo threw a pail of scrub water out the back door without making sure none of the little people were passing by. Surely the water must have hit one of them and made him angry, so it was no surprise when the next day she fell down the stairs."

"He pushed her?" Brian asked.

"Ridiculous!" Aunt Nora said.

"And over in the next county, Mary O'Quinlan was always careful to leave a sip of wine in her glass and some potatoes on the platter out of respect for the little people. But one day her husband's good sense got lost in his stomach. He finished the wine and every scrap of potato. Wouldn't you know that very night the roof began to leak?"

"How can you tell such stories to the boy!" Aunt Nora said.

"Very easily," Grandad answered, "because they truly happened."

Aunt Nora put a hand on Brian's shoulder. "All I can do is explain to your parents that this foolishness is just an old man's way of storytelling."

As she left the kitchen Grandad gave a long sigh. "Being an old man is not something I wished upon myself," he said.

Brian smiled at his great-grandfather. "Tell me more," he said. "Did you ever see any of the little people?"

"That I did," Grandad said. He perked up and began to look happier. "It was a leprechaun. They're a crabby lot, busy making shoes for all the small folk and complaining about everything. Not my favorites, but they do know where the gold is hidden."

"I've read about them," Brian said. "I read that no one can get gold away from a leprechaun."

Grandad's eyes sparkled. "I've heard of a few people who have come away with some coins and none the worse for it. If you catch a leprechaun and hold him tightly he must grant you one wish."

"Did you try to get gold from the leprechaun you saw?"

"No. I did nothing but watch him. He was down in a favorite spot in a grassy ring under the hawthorn trees, behind the bramble bushes and holly hedges, an enchanted place where mortals are not likely to go. It was the music of the faerie flutes that drew me there. There is nothing the little people like better than a party, and surely a party is not a real party without music."

"What do they do at their parties?" Brian asked.

"Feast, of course, and dance. You've never seen dancing like that the little people can do. They'll dress in their finest and kick up their heels and not stop till the first rays of sunlight."

"The leprechaun you saw was dancing?"

"Not him. No, you'll not find a leprechaun admitting in any way that he enjoys life. The one I saw must have left the party. He was walking along, grumbling to himself."

"What about the little people at the party? Did you see them, too?"

"Very few mortals have ever witnessed one of those parties, and on that particular night I was not of a mind to try my luck. I had just bought a new horse, and I didn't want to take any chances on mischief. In fact, just to be on the safe side, I set out a bowl of milk that very night. The little people are fond of milk.

9

They like gold the best, of course, but next to gold a bowl of milk makes them the happiest."

"Did anything happen?"

"Why, the very next day I found a pair of reading glasses that had disappeared six months before, so I knew I had made the right choice."

Grandad leaned so close to Brian that he could smell the faint, wet-bark fragrance of his thin, crinkled skin. And Grandad's clear blue eyes looked into Brian's with such excitement that they seemed to belong to a much younger person—someone who could run and shout and plot mischief—someone Brian's age.

Grandad spoke softly. "You could see a leprechaun, too, if you set about it the right way."

To his surprise, Brian found himself leaning forward and whispering, "What is the right way?"

Grandad winked. "Since we have no gold coins between the two of us, suppose you think about setting out a bowl of milk. A good place to put the bowl would be on the back stoop. If you put it inside the house either Nora or the cat would discover it." He looked around the kitchen and lowered his voice even more. "Keep your thoughts to yourself when the cat's around. Cats live close to magic, so their loyalties are with the little people."

Brian realized he was smiling, because Grandad shook his head and said, "Searching for leprechauns is not something to do for fun. It will take all your imagination and all your powers for quick thinking."

Brian tried to look serious as Grandad added, "You'll have to be very careful, lad. Hunting for a leprechaun can be a risky business!"

For an instant, Brian wished he could trade places with Charlie. Finding a leprechaun would be something Charlie would like to brag about. But Grandad reached out and took Brian's hand, his knobby fingers curling around Brian's. It was like the secret grip of a special pact, something understood only by the two of them. Brian discovered that he really liked this great-grandfather. He was glad they belonged to each other, and that Charlie was thousands of miles away.

Uncle Martin stamped his way into the kitchen, splattering raindrops from his coat. Blossom, the yellow-striped cat, slipped in beside him, streaking out of the way of the big boots, pausing only for a searching stare at Brian before she settled into a warm spot beside the stove. Lady, the sleek-haired brown and white collie mix, shook herself by the door, then noisily crunched at the pan of food which Aunt Nora had set out for her.

"The soft weather is over for a while," Uncle Martin said. "There's even a bit of moon coming out of the clouds. Maybe soon we can go down to the lake for some fishing." For an instant he rested a hand on Grandad's shoulder. "Here's a man who could teach us all more than a bit about fishing. Best fisherman in the county."

Grandad looked pleased. "I might try my hand at that," he said.

"Catch some salmon, and I'll bake it fresh for dinner that very day," Aunt Nora said, as she came into the room. "Now, wash up for supper—all of you."

Brian wanted to laugh out loud as he thought how funny it would be if there really were leprechauns and he actually did catch one and could take it before Aunt Nora. Her eyes would bulge and her mouth would open and shut just like that salmon they were going to catch. She'd never again be able to scold her father for his "foolishness."

"You're looking very pleased with yourself," Aunt Nora said.

"I guess I'm feeling glad to be here," Brian said, surprised that he really was. Salmon fishing, Grandad's stories—this might be an interesting summer, after all.

It wasn't until that night, when he'd been tucked in bed with a hot-water bottle at his feet and a stack of quilts upon him heavy enough to smother the cold air, that Brian remembered the gold-covered chocolate coins that Charlie had given him. He managed to slide from under the quilts and hurried to his suitcase, which was on the floor of the closet. Only the bag of chocolate coins was left in the suitcase, so it was easy to pull one out quickly.

Brian carried the coin to the window, enjoying its glimmer in the bright moonlight, but he didn't stay there long. The fresh air that Aunt Nora insisted was necessary for good health pricked through the open gap above the window sill like millions of sharp icicles. Brian dropped the coin on the sill and hurried back to bed, scrambling under the quilts, clamping his feet on the hot-water bottle, and shivering until his body heat began to warm the hollow in which he lay.

"I wonder," he whispered to himself, grinning into the darkness, "if a leprechaun could be tricked by a gold coin that's really chocolate?"

CHAPTER
TWO

In the morning the sharp cry of a seagull pulled Brian from his dreams. He climbed out of bed, shivering, and hurried to the window, holding back the curtains.

The rain had stopped. A pale, white sun shimmered through the blue haze that hugged the ground, and drops of water from the roof plinked on an overturned bucket that lay under the window sill.

The twisting rock walls, the clumps of wet field grasses, and the plowed furrows that stretched across the side of the hill were separated from Brian by a curtain of magical mist. Here and there grasses softly stirred. Movement began, then stopped as though nothing had happened. Field mice? Maybe a wild rabbit? Brian realized how easy it would be to believe in the little people. This was their land, their mystery, their morning.

Today he'd show his chocolate coin to Grandad. He reached for it, but the coin was gone.

Instinctively he glanced toward the bedroom door, but it was solidly shut with the heavy, never-opened importance that doors seem to have. Surely, no one would have come into his room and taken the coin. Aunt Nora? Uncle Martin? Grandad? Brian shook his head.

But the window was open at least an inch. Not a very big space, but a large enough gap to allow a tiny hand and arm to wiggle through.

"It couldn't be!" Brian whispered.

A fat streak of yellow lighted on a nearby rock wall. Blossom preened one paw with a pink tongue, then stared at Brian with unblinking eyes. Her jaw muscles tightened, her ears twitched, and she looked as though she were laughing at him.

Brian began to shiver and quickly turned away from the window. He dressed as fast as he could, fumbling into his clothes. Even though it was summer, the only really warm room in the house was the kitchen, which was heated by the huge stove that slowly burned blocks of dried peat.

"The peat comes from trees that grew and fell into the boglands, layer upon layer, millions of years ago," Grandad had explained.

Aunt Nora and Grandad smiled at Brian as he came into the kitchen, shutting the door carefully behind him.

"It's a good breakfast you'll be wanting," Aunt

Nora said. "I heard you get up, so it's almost ready."

"After the sun has burned off the mists later in the day, we'll walk to the lake," Grandad said. "You haven't seen our grand Lough Corrib. It has salmon in it like you've never tasted in your life."

Brian wiggled himself into a broad kitchen chair and hiked it up to the table. Aunt Nora placed in front of him a plate of fluffy scrambled eggs; pink ham, frizzled at the edges; and biscuits oozing with butter.

"It looks great," Brian said, "but I don't think I can eat that much."

"Of course you can," Aunt Nora said. "You're a growing boy. Now, what would you like to do this morning?"

"I'd like to help," Brian said, trying to talk around a mouthful of food. At first Aunt Nora looked at him the way his mother did when he talked with his mouth full, but she didn't say anything.

In fact, she began to look pleased. "Chores, is it? Well, there's always something that needs doing. Would you like to feed the horse?"

"Sure!" Brian said, and he began to eat faster.

"We'll send you out to Martin," Grandad said. "He'll put you to work."

"I've never been on a farm before," Brian said. "I've just seen farm animals from the car as we drove past."

"You'll like the horse," Grandad said. "Damon's his name, and he's a fine old fellow. Speak kindly to him

16

and ask him to give your polite regards to the little people. They talk to horses, you know."

"You'll be starting that again, will you?" Aunt Nora said. She picked up Brian's empty plate and nodded to him. "I knew you'd be hungrier than you thought."

"Can I go find Uncle Martin now?" Brian asked.

"I'll get you the proper clothes," Aunt Nora said. "I've still got some of our boys' things put away. They're warm and sturdy, and if they get dirty there's no harm done."

She led Brian into an empty bedroom, and searched through the piles of neatly folded and ironed clothing in the drawers of an old, brown-painted bureau. Finally she found what she wanted and laid the clothes on the bed, giving them a little pat, stroking down the collar of the jacket as though it were an old friend.

"It seems like such a long time since there were young boys in the house," she said in a voice so low that Brian wondered if she were talking to him or to herself. "It was right that they go to the States where they could make more of themselves, and being lonely for them does no good."

"Don't they come to visit you?" Brian asked.

"Oh, yes," she said. She straightened up and plopped the pile of clothing into Brian's arms. "Of course they come, and we've seen their wives and children every year or so, and watched the little ones grow. But it's not the same as if they were living nearby."

"Didn't your sons want to stay in Ireland?" Brian asked.

"I suppose they'd rather have stayed," she said, "but it was important that they have their chance for education, for good jobs and—" She interrupted herself. "Brian, we must recognize that we live in a real world, and that real world demands that we give up certain things."

She walked toward the door, and Brian followed her, clutching the clothing to his chest so he wouldn't drop anything. "Is that why you don't like Grandad to talk about the little people?" he asked.

She stopped and looked at him, shaking her head sadly. "Oh, Brian, there's no room for living in the past with legends of the past. We must work hard to move forward, not waste time in the land of foolish stories."

"Scientists have to study the past, so they can know more about the way things are now," Brian said. "My dad says that in geology—"

"It's not the same thing. Not at all, at all," Aunt Nora said. She moved her arms as though she were sweeping him down the hallway. "Try on these clothes in your room. If necessary, we'll do a bit of fitting, although I think it will just be a matter of turning up cuffs and sleeves."

Brian changed eagerly into the shirt, pants and jacket that were just a bit too big. He hurried back to the kitchen, but Aunt Nora was not in the room.

Grandad winked at Brian. "Take a good look around when you get outside," he said. "You may see something interesting. It's that kind of a morning."

"I know what you mean, Grandad," Brian said. "I looked out the window when I woke up, and I saw the grasses move as though something were there."

Grandad nodded. "There was. There is. Oh, you'll be seeing your leprechaun, Brian." He peered upward into Brian's face. "Have you noticed that our eyes are alike?"

"Blue eyes," Brian said, staring back into his great-grandfather's eyes.

"Not just blue eyes. There's a thin gold ring around the blue, and that makes them special. Special eyes to see special things."

Grandad leaned back in his chair as though he were already tired. "Hurry along. You'll find your uncle Martin still in the pasture. Be careful with Damon."

"Is he dangerous?" Brian was surprised.

"No, but he is an animal. And being so, he's closely in touch with the little people. You would think a horse should know who feeds him and cares for him, but no. His loyalties are to those who live by their magical powers."

"You said to watch out for Blossom, too. Are all the animals like that?"

"Most are," he said, "but not the dog. It's our fine fortune the dog knows who his good friends are."

Brian stopped to button his jacket as he went outside. He stood on the stoop and glanced down at the heavy wooden boards with the gaps between them. There were spaces between the steps. The sides of the stoop were open so that someone not too large could easily crawl underneath. And that someone—if he crouched under the stoop—could reach through the steps.

That was where Grandad suggested he put a bowl of milk for a leprechaun.

"Well," Brian thought, and he had to smile. "Set a trap with milk or chocolate coins? If I haven't anything else to do, I just might use this place as a leprechaun trap."

Brian turned, fastening the last button, and saw Blossom sitting at the foot of the steps, staring at him.

"Hi, Blossom," he said and held out a hand, but the cat kept staring. Brian had the strange feeling that Blossom could read his mind.

He hurried across the lane, climbed the low rock wall, and cut through the field of thick grass and patches of purple clover.

Uncle Martin was in the pasture with the horse. He slipped a bridle over Damon's head. The horse stood stocky-legged, patient except for a brisk nod of his head. His white coat was yellowed with the years, his back broad and strong.

"Will he let me pet him?" Brian asked, as he reached Uncle Martin's side.

Damon stepped back, but Uncle Martin stroked his

head, saying, "There's the fine fellow. There now. Brian's a good lad. He won't harm you, Damon."

The horse stopped and stared right into Brian's eyes. Brian had the strange feeling that Damon, too, was trying to read his mind, so he thought about what a great thing it would be to have a horse like Damon and ride him to school and say to Charlie, "I bet you've never done that."

Damon seemed to relax. He bent his head to nuzzle the grass as though he'd forgotten now that Brian was there. Brian was able to stroke his nose. "Could I ride him?" he asked Uncle Martin.

"Sometime," Uncle Martin said, "although he's not much of a horse for riding. He's a good workhorse instead."

"I came to help you," Brian said. "Could I feed him?"

"Tonight you may, because old Damon's already had his fill. How would you like to help Lady take the sheep to the pasture on the hill? She'll do her job. You'll just open and close the gates for her."

"That's easy," Brian said.

Uncle Martin smiled. "It's good to be having another pair of hands to help out."

"I guess Grandad can't do the farm work now, can he?" Brian asked.

"We each do what we can," Uncle Martin said. "In his time there was no one in the county who worked harder than himself. That's not something to be forgetting."

Damon dropped his head, blowing his warm breath against Brian's cheek. Brian reached up and stroked the horse's side. "Uncle Martin, does Grandad really believe his stories about the little people?"

Damon drew back with a snort as Uncle Martin said, "Indeed he does. He's a man of honor and not one for telling that which he knows to be untrue."

"Then you believe in them, too?"

"That's not what I said." Uncle Martin whistled to Lady, and the dog bounded across the field toward him. "It's not the kind of thing I've had time to give much thought to."

"Aunt Nora doesn't like Grandad to tell the stories."

"It could be she takes it all a bit too serious." Uncle Martin held out a hand to Lady, who immediately sat by his side, waiting for her next command. "Nora's been a good daughter to her father, the more credit to her," he added. "Now—are you ready to work with Lady?"

The morning unfolded as Brian climbed behind the dozen long-haired sheep, watching the dog, Lady. She moved to the left and the right, sometimes nudging, sometimes nipping, keeping the sheep in their direction up the hill. Lady was doing the work. All Brian was needed for was to close and latch the gate once the sheep were in the high meadow.

23

He stumbled over one of the outcrops of rock that pushed through the grasses. The land was hard and stony under its cover of green. He whistled to Lady as the last ewe entered the meadow; and when the dog ran to him, he closed and latched the gate.

As he turned to look down the hill he gasped. Before him lay a glimmer of golds and greens. The air was more golden than the clumps of flowering gorse. And the clear finger of the lake that could be seen behind the trees at the foot of the hill was covered with a skim of glitter. He was surrounded by greens of every hue, from the yellow green grasses that lay in the sunlight, to the deep blue green patches under the shadows of tattered clouds.

It was not the same land as that he had seen in the mists of morning. The little people seemed far away. Now was a time for running, for exploring, for fishing. Brian unbuttoned his jacket and raced down the hill, Lady excitedly barking at this new game. He hoped Grandad was ready to go to the lake.

They met at the door. "I was watching for you," Grandad said.

As they walked down the lane, Brian matched his pace with his great-grandfather's shorter steps. "Did you keep your eyes open this morning?" Grandad asked.

"I guess not," Brian said. "I was watching the sheep and the way Lady works. I wasn't thinking about the little people."

"I can understand that," Grandad said. "Everything is new to you. It probably hasn't even entered your mind to wonder why a leprechaun is easier to come across than a pooka, or a banshee, or a ginger-haired faerie."

"A what?" Brian stopped and stared at Grandad.

"Here is a fine shortcut to the lake," Grandad said, suddenly turning to the right and entering a tunnel of beech and elm trees. There was a narrow footpath and a thin, silver stream that slid over moss-covered rocks. Brian followed him, pulling his jacket a little tighter in the chill of the deep shade.

"It's because leprechauns are so busy grumbling and complaining and counting their gold coins over and over again, they forget to keep their wits about them and watch out for mortals," Grandad said.

Brian looked to both sides. He felt as though they were being watched. "What's a pooka?" he asked Grandad. "And those other things?"

"A pooka is a creature of the night," Grandad said. "He sometimes appears as an eagle, a goat, or a bat. But mostly he comes as a fiery black horse with burning yellow eyes, breathing flames. The best thing to do is to keep your eyes on the ground as he passes, lest he fling you on his back and ride with you through the night until he drops you into a ditch."

He stopped and took some deep breaths. It was so still in the glen that the only sound was the slushing of the water over the rocks.

"Banshees are attached to the very old Irish families who are related to the early heroes. They appear when someone in those families dies. Many a person in the quiet of the night has suddenly heard the wailing and mourning of a banshee. When you hear a banshee, say a quick prayer."

"Are the faeries like Tinkerbell in Peter Pan?" Brian asked.

"Tinkerbell!" Grandad's eyes opened wide. "Why, she's not a true faerie! She's not even a poor relation! Irish faeries often take the shape of mortals and are hard to detect. But you can spot the best of them by their ginger-colored hair. Always speak politely, show no fear, and wish them a good day. Are you ready to be moving along, now that you've had your rest?"

Brian wanted to laugh, but he just nodded. His great-grandfather was one of the most interesting people he'd ever met.

"Then come along," Grandad said, "and when we get to the lake I'll tell you how to hear a leprechaun coming."

It didn't take long to reach the lake. The tunnel widened, and the pathway led to a grassy knoll that rolled down to the water's edge.

"The water is so blue!" Brian said.

"Blue when it's not gray, and gray when it's not green," Grandad said. "The water is a mirror to the sky." He led the way to an outcropping of large rocks

26

near the water's edge. "You can sit up here with me if you like," he said. "The grass is softer, but it's too damp for old bones."

Brian climbed up to the top of the rocks and looked down at his great-grandfather. "Tell me," he said, "how do you hear a leprechaun coming?" It sounded like the kind of joke that he and Charlie liked to tell each other, and he laughed.

Grandad was solemn. "It's not a time for laughter," he said. "It's a well-known truth. Listen. Then tell me what you hear."

Brian listened. He was used to hearing traffic, or the sound of a radio, or an airplane, or people talking. "I don't hear anything," he told Grandad.

"Close your eyes," Grandad said. "If it was real listening you were doing, you'd surely have mentioned the patting of the water against the shore, and the crack of a twig that dropped from the elm nearby, and the rustle of new leaves as the wind passed through."

Brian closed his eyes again and waited. A strange thing happened. It was as though he had become a part of the rock itself, because he began to hear a rhythm of sounds: little rustlings, a swish that might have been the wings of a heron in flight, the steady lapping of the water. The sounds moved like a kind of music. Across the lake a bird trilled, and even its song slid smoothly into the pattern.

"Yes," Brian whispered to Grandad, as he opened

his eyes. "Everything is in time with everything else."

Grandad grinned. "This is the way of nature. The animals understand it and live by its rules. But leprechauns, too intent upon themselves, are out of time. The biggest of them is no more than two feet high, and they weigh less than nothing at the most. But you can hear them coming, because they are a sound out of place."

Brian hugged his knees. Lots of people believed in ghosts. If there were such things as ghosts, then why couldn't there be leprechauns and pookas and all the other things Grandad had talked about? He shivered. He'd never want to run into a pooka! Not even Charlie would want to meet a pooka.

"If you come up with a plan for finding a leprechaun, better it be kept a secret between you and yourself until after it's done," Grandad said.

"You wouldn't want me to tell you about it?"

Grandad shook his head. "I've told you what I know that will help you on your way to seeing one of the little men, but remember they've spent more years than we can count outwitting the likes of you and me."

Brian climbed down from the rocks, and Grandad gripped his arm, leaning heavily as they walked. His steps were slow but firm, and he said, "It's best I help you along this path, lad. We'll not be wanting you to stumble."

Brian wished he could tell his great-grandfather how glad he was to be with him, how happy he was that they had found each other. But he didn't know how to put his feelings into words. Maybe there'd be something he could do to show Grandad how he felt. That would be even better.

CHAPTER
THREE

During the next week Brian worked with Uncle Martin, and twice they went fishing in mornings so early and clear that the sounds of the lake and the hills thrummed their soft rhythm to anyone who would listen. Uncle Martin was not much for talking, but Brian was comfortable just sitting near him, sharing the excitement of their flopping, wiggling catch.

He wished that Grandad had come with them, but on both occasions his great-grandfather had begged off.

"At his age he has a right to stay by the fire," Uncle Martin had told Brian, and Brian, shivering in spite of the warm coat he had borrowed, understood.

Ireland was cold, even in the summer. He was always glad for the warmth of the kitchen, and often wished, when he headed for the layers of quilts on his bed and the hot-water bottle wrapped in a towel, that he could sleep in the kitchen. Old Blossom, curled next to the stove, had the warmest bed in the house.

Each day was brushed with the magic of Grandad's stories about Ireland's mystical inhabitants who dwell in the secret clefts and glens of the land, avoiding both those who believe and those who do not believe; playing their thin, sweet music, feasting and fighting where mortals will not go—in the ruins of old castles and abandoned graveyards. Brian learned how the faeries create their own fiery steeds from nothing but a bit of straw or a blade of grass, and how they ride these horses faster than gusts of winter wind that howl from the north.

Grandad made the stories so real that Brian could feel them, and they seemed to sing in his mind long after Aunt Nora would bustle into the kitchen to begin preparing the meals. For Grandad was careful not to begin his stories in the hearing of Aunt Nora. And only once, as her footsteps tapped through the next room on her way toward the kitchen, did he lean toward Brian and say, "Have you thought of a plan to see your leprechaun yet?"

"I'll think about it," Brian had answered. "I really will. So far I've been kind of busy."

There were letters from his mother—quickly scribbled notes that told about lectures and meetings and ended with how much they missed him. There was even a letter from Charlie, who had gone to Washington, D.C., with his parents and seen the White House.

He claimed that the President came out of his office and waved at him. Brian managed to write a letter to his parents and sent Charlie a post card. He didn't mention the President.

One evening Brian followed Uncle Martin into the house after the evening chores. On a peg near the kitchen door, he hung his jacket. He washed quickly, hungry for supper, even though his plate had been piled high at the midday meal. He tried not to gulp down the lamb stew Aunt Nora had made, and he helped her wash the dishes. He knew how surprised his mother would be that no one had even had to ask him.

"You're a fine lad," Aunt Nora said as she wrung out the dish cloth and hung it to dry.

Grandad spoke up. "Nora, you were always good about offering with the chores, too. I mind that on the nights we walked into town to hear the words of the storyteller, you would always tidy the kitchen before we started out."

"That's because I always put first things first," Nora answered. She bustled about, smoothing her apron and hanging it up, but Brian could see she was pleased.

"Well I remember you then, with your hair that had captured the color of sunset, all pulled back with a ribbon around it. You'd run down the lane after your brothers, stopping only to scold the dog who wanted to follow." He chuckled. "You were a pretty child with your wide eyes and your solemn ways."

"And a pretty woman." Uncle Martin's voice was as soft as his smile.

"Go on with you," Aunt Nora laughed.

No matter how he tried, Brian couldn't picture his great-aunt as a child or even a young woman. But he liked the happiness in the kitchen, and he wanted to know more about the storyteller. "Aunt Nora," he said, "do you remember some of the stories you heard when you were young?"

"Of course I do," she said.

"Then, could you tell them to me?"

"I'm not a storyteller. I couldn't tell them the same way." Aunt Nora looked embarrassed. "Besides, they were nothing but a lot of superstitious, frightening foolishness."

Grandad spoke up. "Nora, girl, you'd be a good storyteller, if you gave it half a try. Pull up your chair, and we'll take turns telling our tales. Just like in the old days."

"Great!" Brian said. "That would be fun!"

Aunt Nora actually slapped her hand down on the table top. She pulled it away as though it had been burned, but it was her cheeks that had turned red. "We are not going to fill the lad's head with silly make-believe, born out of ignorance! I don't want him telling his parents that's all he learned from us. The little people do not exist, and it's time we all accepted that fact!"

She flipped on the television set that rested on a

small table against the whitewashed wall, and stared at it as though she were determined nothing more be said.

The room was silent. Aunt Nora and Uncle Martin sat back in their wooden kitchen chairs, as they did most evenings, watching whatever programs appeared on the channel. But Brian peered through the corners of his eyes at his great-grandfather.

Grandad slumped in his chair. He was staring at the tips of his shoes, not the television set. Brian wanted to reach out and hold him, to tell him not to worry, that he believed.

His eyes opened wide as he realized what he had thought. That he believed? Well, why not? No one had really proved there were no such things as leprechauns, and Grandad insisted they did exist, because he had seen one. There had to be something out there. Brian had felt whispering sounds, too silent to be heard, and seen riffles moving the wrong way through the gently quivering grasses. Little people? They were part of the history and heritage of this country—part of the same heritage that was Brian's, too.

Brian looked at his Aunt Nora, who seemed to be stiffened with steel and springs even when she was relaxing. He didn't understand her. She had been nice enough to him, but there was something unbending about her. Brian would love to plop a leprechaun down before Aunt Nora and say "Here's the proof.

Now stop telling Grandad that his stories are foolish."

"I'll do it!" he said to himself. "I won't just try to see a leprechaun. I'll actually catch one."

Something brushed against his leg, and he looked down to see Blossom staring up at him, her eyes widening, then scrunching into little gold slits.

"Blossom," he thought, "if you can read minds, then read this—scat!"

Blossom jumped and ran to her spot next to the stove.

That's all that Blossom would get from him, Brian thought. He already knew what he'd do, and he'd keep it out of his mind and away from the cat.

He impatiently squirmed in his chair until finally Aunt Nora said, "Well now, it's time for us to be getting to bed." She turned off the television set.

Uncle Martin opened the door and whistled for Lady, who slipped in quickly and curled up on the other side of the stove, ignoring Blossom, who opened just one eye to watch the dog's progress.

Brian stood up and stretched. "I think I'll stay up a while and have a glass of milk."

Aunt Nora shrugged. "Just don't stay up too late. A growing boy needs his rest."

"Goodnight, lad," Grandad said, and his eyes twinkled with a secret shared. Grandad would know what Brian was going to do.

As soon as the door to the hallway closed firmly

behind them, Brian got the milk from the refrigerator and poured it carefully into a small blue bowl he found in the cupboard. He pulled his jacket from the peg by the outside door and put it on. Slowly and carefully he carried the bowl of milk outside and placed it on the stoop, making sure that Blossom was tucked in her place beside the stove. Brian turned out the kitchen light, erasing the yellow square that spilled from the window. The darkness which gobbled the space was so deep and thick that Brian had to feel his way down the steps, around the side, and under the stoop.

He sat without moving, hugging his knees under his chin. He tried to pretend that the cold wasn't seeping through the wool of the jacket, poking straight through to his bones like tiny needles. As his eyes began to adjust to the darkness, deep, hulking shapes loomed out of the night: the barn, the shed, treetops that shuddered slightly in the light breeze. Shredded clouds trailed across the moon, which blinked its feeble light.

It would be hard to see a leprechaun coming, but Grandad had taught him to hear one. Brian closed his eyes, listening intently.

Slowly he began to pick up the pattern of sounds in the night: the wind movements, the rustlings of grass, the steady chirp of a cricket by the lane, the leaves whispering against the sky. The rhythm, the beat, in time, in time.

Suddenly he heard a movement that was out of step. The sound came closer with an uneven patter, like that made by small feet. The lowest board creaked.

"It's now or never!" Brian whispered. His right hand shot out, groping until he touched something thin and bony and warm. His fingers closed around it, clutching it tightly. "I've got you!" he shouted.

A terrible screech hurt his ears, and what felt like a leg jerked and leaped in his hand. But Brian hung on. With a clatter the bowl tipped, and cold milk poured down through the cracks between the boards and onto Brian's head. Brian held the leg tightly through all the racket. He had caught a leprechaun, and he wasn't going to let go.

The kitchen light came on, and the back door flew open. Lady barked furiously.

"What's happening out here?" Aunt Nora called. Without taking time for an answer she added, "Brian! Why are you down there, and what are you doing to Blossom?"

"I've caught a leprechaun!" Brian shouted.

"You've caught the cat!" she shouted back.

Brian let go. He saw something streak around the corner of the house. He crawled out from under the stoop, wiping milk from his eyes. "I thought it was a leprechaun," he said.

"What nonsense," Aunt Nora said. "And what a

waste of good milk. Come inside this very minute, Brian!"

Uncle Martin and Grandad were in the kitchen. Grandad was dressed, but Uncle Martin was trying to stuff his pajama top into his trousers. He hobbled into the room with one shoe off and one on.

"Are you all right, Brian?" he asked. "It looks as though the cat gave you a couple of scratches."

Brian stared at his hand. There were a few scratches, none of them deep, but they began to hurt.

"I'll fix those," Aunt Nora said, "and we'll wash the milk out of your hair." She pressed her lips together in a thin line and scowled at Grandad.

"It's you who should be blamed," she said, "for filling the boy's head with such foolishness."

"It's not Grandad's fault," Brian said. "He didn't know I was going to try to catch a leprechaun."

"Now, now, Nora," Grandad said. "No real harm was done."

"No harm? It's a good thing we have no near neighbors, or they'd think we'd all been murdered in our beds!" She dabbed at Brian's hand with something that stung.

Brian had his mouth open to tell her he was sorry when he glanced at the floor near the stove. Blossom squinted up at him through shining slits. She looked smug with the thoughts she was having.

"There's Blossom!" Brian cried.

"Of course she's there," Aunt Nora said. "That's her spot every night."

"But you said Blossom was out on the porch!"

"And she was, with you hanging on to the poor frightened creature's leg."

"That cat ran off," Brian said.

"Nonsense. It's there she is." Aunt Nora poured some warm water from the kettle into a basin. "Now rinse off that milk. Here's some soap for your hair."

"Grandad," Brian began, "if Blossom were in the house, then—"

But Aunt Nora held up her hand. "We'll have no more talk tonight," she said. "We'll all be getting back to bed."

Tomorrow, Brian thought. Tomorrow he and Grandad could talk about what had happened. That wasn't Blossom he had grabbed in the dark. It had to be a leprechaun. And if it were, then the little man had outwitted him, as Grandad said he'd probably do. But the contest wasn't over yet. He'd work out another plan, so that he could bring a leprechaun to Aunt Nora and say, "Grandad was right."

There had to be a way.

CHAPTER
FOUR

In the morning a cold, gray fog clung to the land. Brian shivered and drew close to the fragrant peat fire in the iron stove. The peat made him think of forests and glens and places he had never been. The thought startled him. How could he feel so close to something he didn't know?

"A spell of bad weather come upon us," Aunt Nora said to herself, as she poured a heaping cup of oatmeal into a large pot of boiling water.

"It's not surprising," Grandad said.

"If your tools are handy after breakfast, could you fix the rung on the black oak chair?" she asked her father. "One of the legs has suddenly turned wobbly."

He nodded and looked at Brian. "It's not surprising," he repeated.

Aunt Nora turned from the stove, and Brian stared at his feet. Grandad had said the little people shouldn't be crossed, and he had upset one of them.

"Listen to me," Aunt Nora said, waving her long wooden spoon. "Leprechauns had nothing to do with this."

"Can you prove that they didn't?" Grandad asked.

"Well now, can you prove that they did?" she answered.

"No, so there we are back to the beginning. But just a word of advice for Brian. You were a bit too bold in grabbing his leg as you did. Just watch. Just listen. There's no need to make one of them angry."

"Oh, Da." Aunt Nora laid her spoon on the side of the stove and knelt by her father, resting her hands on his arms. "Brian and his parents come from a country where people prize education. They would all turn their mouths down for sure at those who spoke with ignorance and superstition."

"It is the unbelievers like you who have nearly driven the little people away from the rightful bond they should have with humans," he answered.

"The little people are not real."

He leaned toward her, their faces almost touching. "Are you forgetting, Nora, girl, all that was taught you when you were young?"

"They were stories, Da. That's all they were."

"You liked the stories."

"I hated the stories!" She stood, moving slowly and stiffly, rubbing her lower back for a moment. "Those stories terrified me, and there was many a night I lay in the darkness with the words whirling in my mind, too frightened to even cry out."

"Nora, girl," he said. "It's not once that you've told me. I could have let you know that you were in no harm. If the little people—"

"No more!" Aunt Nora said. She picked up the spoon and waved it, tapping it against her left hand. "Forget that make-believe world. There are no little people, and it's best we'd be remembering that."

Grandad's wrinkled forehead puckered into a frown. It seemed more important than ever now to Brian that he bring a leprechaun before Aunt Nora and say, "See! Grandad was right!"

During breakfast Uncle Martin invited Brian to help him in the barn. Aunt Nora provided a slicker to put over his jacket, and Brian eagerly followed his father's uncle to the barn.

It loomed through the fog like a giant haystack, shapeless and dark. The mists clung to Brian's face in wet patches, running in droplets down his cheeks like cold tears. He felt as though he were walking through a blanket. Yet under that blanket there were stirrings and murmurings and small rustling noises from things he could not see. He hurried his steps so that he was closer to Uncle Martin.

The door of the barn was rough and solid to his touch, and the mists that tried to creep inside were shut out as Uncle Martin closed the wide door.

43

Damon raised his head and stared at them. Again, Brian had the uncomfortable feeling that Damon was trying to read his mind. He thought of sun on the fields and riding Damon's broad back as the horse stepped over stones and tufts of primroses.

Damon studied him for a moment, blinked sleepily, and turned his head away.

"We keep the hay in a loft overhead," Uncle Martin said. "Would you like to climb the ladder up to the loft and throw down some hay to me?"

"Will I be able to lift it?" Brian asked. He remembered the big bales of hay that had decorated the school auditorium when they had a square dance program for the parents.

Uncle Martin chuckled. "Some of it is loose. There's a pitchfork I use to pick it up and drop it down here, but you can use your arms to do it, if the fork's too heavy."

Brian took off his slicker and laid it nearby on top of some boxes. He climbed the wooden ladder, stopping as the floor of the loft came into view. He peered into the dimness and thought what a great hiding place it would be.

"Just a step or two more," Uncle Martin reminded him. Brian hurried up into the loft. He scooped up armfuls of the scratchy hay and dropped them below. His shoulders and back began to hurt, and he wondered if Uncle Martin would ever tell him it was enough.

Finally the welcome words came: "That's a fine job, Brian. You're a good lad."

Brian stopped to rest and rubbed his nose. It itched from the pungent smell of the hay. He looked around the loft. It was dark under the rafters, and he didn't want to think about spiders who might be watching him. Something was watching him. He could feel it. He stared into the rafters, but saw only the dark shadows. The feeling must have come from his imagination, because no one was in the loft with him. No one and nothing that he could see.

Hay was spread over the wooden planks, and he could lie here and watch for a leprechaun in perfect comfort. Grandad had said that animals and little people were friendly with each other. What if he put the bowl of milk in the barn tonight and hid in the loft? A leprechaun would feel at ease with the horse nearby. While the little man was busy drinking the milk, Brian could scramble down the ladder and grab him!

And suppose he put a chocolate coin next to the milk? A double trap? He grinned.

"Are you coming down now, Brian?" Uncle Martin called. "You might like to help me care for the leather straps and harness."

Brian climbed down the ladder. He jumped the last rung to the floor, turning as he did. He found himself face to face with Blossom, who was curled on top of his slicker, watching him carefully from half-closed eyes.

"It's the cat!" he said.

"Old Blossom?" Uncle Martin smiled. "She's trying to get used to you, I guess. She's been that curious about what you've been up to in the loft. She's watched your every move."

Brian didn't like the feeling that Blossom somehow knew what he was thinking. So he thought about small, plump field mice scrambling through the tall grass. Blossom began to stretch and arch her back. In a moment she ran to the door and cried to be let out.

"Do Irish cats read minds?" Brian asked Uncle Martin. He shut the door behind Blossom, glad to see her go.

"That's a question for your grandad," Uncle Martin said. "He's the one who's up on those things. Just don't ask your aunt Nora." He looked toward the house. "Nora's always had to work hard and make a little go a long way. She's raised two good sons and made a home for her father. It may not seem like it to someone who doesn't know Nora well, but there's a lot of love in her. Sure, it's a bit set in her ways she is, no doubt about it, but perhaps she's earned that right."

He handed Brian a bridle and a soft rag. "Rub hard. It's good for the leather to stay clean and soft."

Brian sat on one of the boxes. He looked at the horse as he worked. He thought about sugar lumps and crunchy apples, but Damon ignored him. What made him think animals could read his mind? Brian wondered. He decided he had let his imagination go too far.

The fog lasted through the afternoon. Grandad now and then glanced out the window and nodded as though the bad weather was something to expect. It gave Brian the strange feeling that the thick, gray haze hung only over their house and land, and the rest of the world was filled with sunshine.

He could see that all the days of this family of his father's were very much the same. They rose early. They worked hard at the many chores they each had to do. They watched television in the kitchen, the room filled with steamy warmth from the evening meal. And they went to bed early. One day moved into another that was like it, and another and another.

But Grandad's days were more interesting, because he had the little people to think about. Brian turned out his bedroom light that night and stood at the window. He shivered, staring eagerly into the darkness. He wondered if one of the little people might be out there staring in at him.

It wouldn't be long until they met—he and a leprechaun. He would pick a night when the soft weather had passed and there was moonlight to show the way. This time his plan was going to work.

A few days later Brian knew it was time. When he was sure everyone must be asleep, he tucked another chocolate coin into his pocket and poured milk into a bowl. He put on his jacket and gloves and left the house silently, carrying the bowl carefully and moving the outside kitchen door open just an inch at a time so it wouldn't squeak.

"Don't you dare move," he whispered to Blossom, who settled herself more snugly next to the stove and wouldn't look at him.

Clouds suddenly appeared, sifting the moonlight into useless glitter. Brian had little help as he felt his way across the lumpy ground and over the path to the barn. Now and then he stopped, listening. Night sounds were louder than day sounds. He could hear the tune and rhythm of the chirrups and snicks of insects, and cracklings of dying leaves, and whisperings of sleepy birds.

Step by step. Carefully. Cautiously. And there was the barn, a mound in front of his face. He reached for the door with one groping hand. He found the latch and opened it.

As Brian entered the barn a sudden streak of moonlight brightened the window, making it possible for him to see Damon in his stall and the ladder stretching to the loft. The horse snuffled, his warm breath in the cold air like clouds of steam from a kettle. Brian put the bowl of milk and the chocolate coin on the floor near the foot of the ladder.

Damon whinnied softly. It sounded like a laugh.

"Be quiet, Damon," Brian whispered.

With Damon watching him, Brian climbed the ladder and stretched out on the straw. He shivered in the chill, still air, but he was glad he was cold. It would keep him from falling asleep.

Brian waited, listening. The night sounds slipped into a pattern again. Even the clump of Damon's hooves against the packed earth and the sound of his heavy body against the walls of the stall fit into the rhythm. The heartbeat of night was soothing in its own way. Brian's heart beat with it, and his eyes kept closing as he fought to stay awake.

At first he thought it was part of a dream. Something had broken the rhythm. A low muttering slid into what sounded like spoken words: "So he's up there, is he?"

"You can believe it." A deep voice throbbed under a whinny.

Brian shook his head, trying to clear it. Part of his mind told him he had heard two voices. But another part of his mind insisted it was only the scratching of straw on the stable floor and the whinny of the horse.

He crept close to the edge of the loft and peered over, but at that moment a cloud completely covered the moon, and it was impossible for Brian to see beyond the shadows.

"If there's a leprechaun down there, don't move!" Brian yelled. He didn't take time to think. He grabbed for the top of the ladder and swung over the edge of the loft.

In the next few seconds he wondered if he had tripped over his own feet or if something had happened to the once-sturdy rungs of the ladder. Sliding, clutching, grabbing, and scrambling, Brian fell down the ladder. He landed on his feet, tripped over the bowl of milk with a great clatter, and sat down on the packed earth floor so hard that he shouted, "Ouch!"

Damon laughed again with a long, high-pitched whinny, and Brian could hear Lady barking inside the house. He twisted to look in every direction, but there was no leprechaun in sight—only Blossom.

He heard the sound of the back door opening and closing. He could hear his Uncle Martin's voice and the shrill, excited chatter of Aunt Nora.

"Who's out there?" Uncle Martin called.

"I am!" Brian shouted back.

He got to his feet, rubbing his sore legs as the barn door opened, and blinked in the beam from Uncle Martin's flashlight.

"What in the world are you doing out here?" Aunt Nora cried. She saw the overturned bowl and the spilled milk. "Not again! It's looking for a leprechaun you were!"

"I tried to catch him," Brian said.

She clutched her robe more tightly around her body. Wisps of gray hair stuck out from her head, making her look prickly. "Grandad has filled your head full of nonsense! Brian, why must you do these things?"

"Because," Brian said, "I have to prove to you that Grandad isn't a foolish old man."

Aunt Nora's eyes glistened, and Brian realized they were brimming with tears. "Oh, no. It's not a foolish old man that he is," she whispered. "It's his stories —only the silly tales, but not Da."

"I want you to believe in him, to believe that he's right."

She shook her head and stood a little straighter, a little taller. "I wouldn't believe in leprechauns unless I saw one myself, and that will never happen."

Uncle Martin's hand was firm on Brian's shoulder. "It's late," he said. "Let's be off to bed and a warm hot-water bottle in the sheets."

"The chocolate coin!" Brian twisted to search the flooring.

"What are you looking for?" Uncle Martin asked.

"My coin," Brian said. "I put one of my chocolates that look like gold next to the bowl of milk. It's gone."

Aunt Nora sighed. "Next you'll be telling me a leprechaun took it."

"But maybe—" Brian began.

"Surely in all this excitement it's been kicked under the straw or into a corner." Uncle Martin's voice was as calm as always, and he smiled at Brian. "The mice will be having a treat, I'm thinking. Come along now, Brian."

Brian followed Aunt Nora as she marched from the

barn. Uncle Martin was behind him. No one said another word. It was certainly clear enough to Brian that his aunt Nora didn't like his searching for leprechauns, but she hadn't said he couldn't. Brian was more determined than ever to catch a leprechaun and march him right under her nose. His time was running out as the days moved past, but he'd never give up until he had caught one!

CHAPTER
FIVE

In the morning Aunt Nora gave Brian what she called a "proper scolding." She talked without stopping for at least fifteen minutes about the possibility of broken bones, of being stepped on by the horse, of lying injured in the darkness, and of scaring them all witless. Brian meekly apologized. He decided it would be much safer not to mention leprechauns around Aunt Nora—at least until he had one in hand to show her.

For he had another plan. It had come to him as he lay in bed before falling asleep.

He had been looking in the wrong places. He had tried to lure a leprechaun with bowls of milk and chocolate coins, and the small man had been wary. How much better it would be to hunt for a leprechaun in the little man's own territory, where he would feel safe, where he wouldn't suspect Brian's presence.

Grandad had talked of holly hedges and hawthorn trees and grassy rings. If Brian did some exploring he was sure he would find the right spot. And he would keep his thoughts from everyone—especially Blossom. He was sure she had drilled into his secret ideas with those slitted eyes like yellow beams of light.

Brian knew he had to succeed soon. The milk had suddenly soured, and a plate had fallen from the table and cracked in two. He couldn't go on upsetting the little people and have nothing to show for it.

During the next few mornings as he worked with Uncle Martin, now and then Brian would glance down the hillsides, searching for circular plantings of trees that might mean secret rings of magic. In the afternoons he walked the lanes with Grandad, sometimes leaving him to rest and chat with an old friend, as Brian prowled the thickets and glens alone.

He ate Aunt Nora's fine meals with a hunger he had never had before, and he proudly carried home his fish from Lough Corrib and grinned at her praise. The work clothes he wore began to fit; and when he looked in the old, darkened mirror that hung over the bathroom wash basin, he could see that his freckles had multiplied and under them his skin was tanned.

The weeks were passing quickly. Brian had searched for likely leprechaun country everywhere he went, and it hadn't helped. "Grandad," he finally said, "tell me more about the little people and where to find them." But he kept his plan to himself.

"It could be that telling is not as good as showing,"

Grandad said. "We'll take a stroll after the noon meal."

And as soon as the meal was over and the plates had been carried to the sink, Grandad pushed his chair back from the kitchen table and said, "It's such a grand day the whole world should be outside enjoying it. Brian, we'll walk in a new direction. There's a small castle you must see."

Aunt Nora put down the spoons she was holding. "Surely, it's not those ruins near Corrib that you mean. It's much too far for you to walk."

"Ah, Nora, it's not too far."

"And there are hills. The hills will tire you."

"If I get tired I'll sit a while," Grandad said. "But a ruined castle, no matter where, is never too far for a young boy to walk."

"A real castle?" Brian asked.

"It was at one time," Uncle Martin said.

"It will always be to those who once lived there," Grandad said.

Uncle Martin smiled, but Aunt Nora shrugged. "Suit yourself," she said. "If you get tired, stop and rest, and look for a ride back, though there's not many use that back road you'll no doubt be taking."

"I've never seen a castle!" Brian said.

"Then let's be off," Grandad said.

Brian got their jackets and followed Grandad as he led the way down the back steps and across the field to a narrow paved road that curled over the hill. They walked slowly, but as they crested the hill the road sloped gently downward, and Grandad stepped up the pace.

The hills were carpeted in sweeping shades of green that moved as the clouds moved. Brian could hear the splash of a hidden stream and smell the sweet-sour fragrance of the bee-sucked blossoms of the gorse.

"Ireland is a beautiful country, Grandad," Brian said.

"Yes," Grandad said. "And most of all in these quiet places which are kept that way by the little people."

They entered a tunnel of tree branches tangled over their heads. The stream gurgled near their feet. Now and then Grandad stopped to rest, and Brian kept his eyes open. Somewhere, somehow he must find one of the magic circles that was home to the little people.

Finally Grandad said, "There is the fine stump of a tree just made for resting. If I'm not mistaken, it was here that old John Flynn saw a pooka thundering along the road, but he sat quietly and kept his eyes on the ground, and the pooka passed him by without so much as a glance. So that's where I'll wait while you go to the castle."

"I could wait with you," Brian said, "in case a pooka comes along."

"Pookas only travel by night," Grandad said.

"Oh," Brian said, embarrassed to find he had given a sigh of relief. "Then I'll go on to the castle."

"It's not wrong to be afraid of a pooka." Grandad tilted his head and studied Brian. "In fact, if you go into the land belonging to the little people and your intentions are not to their liking, it's almost sure you'll meet up with a pooka, wish it or not."

Brian looked over his shoulder for just an instant. "Why?" he whispered.

"Because the beings who live in the world of magic must band with each other for protection against the world of humans."

"I wouldn't hurt a leprechaun."

"Of course you wouldn't, but how are they to know that—the ginger-haired faeries and the banshees and the pookas?"

"All of them?" Brian gulped. "But I only want—"

Grandad held a finger to his lips and glanced into the shadows. "There's a price to be paid for everything that is gained, Brian. Do you understand?"

Brian nodded.

Grandad's eyes twinkled again. "However, just taking a wee look shouldn't bother the little people."

Brian tried to keep his plan to catch a leprechaun out of his thoughts. Surely the little people wouldn't object to what he was going to do. At least, he hoped they wouldn't.

"I have things to think about, and so do you," Grandad added. "So keep on the road and in about half a mile you'll come to the castle. Don't be afraid to climb around and take a good look. That's what castle ruins are for."

"Will you be all right here, by yourself?" Brian asked.

"Except for having to admit to myself that your aunt Nora was right, I'll be fine," Grandad said. "Go along, and take your time. I'll be here when you come back this way."

Brian walked faster over the road. A small car chugged past him, and the driver waved. Brian wondered what would happen on that narrow road if two cars were to meet. One would probably have to back up. In a way he was glad he had seen another person. He wasn't exactly afraid of the creatures Grandad had talked about, because the sunlight would keep them at a distance; but he felt uncomfortable knowing that at some time in the future they might try to get in his way.

The road curved in a great sweep that carried it through the trees to the lakeshore where the tower of a small lookout castle stood like a stiff sentinel. Long grasses and thick bramble bushes had crept in to carpet some of its roofless rooms. There was a stair that led to nowhere and arches with nothing left to support, their former walls a tumble of square-cut gray stones.

Brian climbed and crawled and peered into dark places. He wished Charlie were here to share this with him. He knew Charlie had never been in a castle—even one in ruins. Brian explored every foot of the small castle except for the parts protected with the prickly holly and bramble.

"Bramble," he whispered. "And a holly hedge!" Carefully he leaned to part the holly, watching for the thorn-edged leaves. He stepped forward, lost his balance, and found himself sliding and rolling a few feet down a short incline into a small, grassy area.

He sat up and looked around. It was a perfect circle, ringed closely with hawthorn trees!

"I've found it!" he gasped. He waited, not moving. He watched. He listened. It didn't take long to realize that no one was here but himself. If this place belonged to the little people they were away for the moment.

Brian climbed back to the spot he had fallen through, where the bushes parted easily over the gap. He was careful not to disturb anything inside or around the hideaway. It would be easy to find again. The castle was the landmark; and at the spot in the hedge Brian placed a small triangle of stones, something so small that no one would notice. But he would know it was there, and it would help him find the exact place again. There was just one thing he'd need: a moonlit night, so that he could find his way.

But on this moonlit night, would there be pookas who would thunder toward him? And banshees whose wails would freeze his bones? And ginger-haired faeries who would use their magic on him? Brian shuddered. "*If* I come back here," he whispered into the silence.

Slowly he walked back to the tree stump where his great-grandfather was waiting, wrapped in late afternoon shadows, blending into the forest as though he were a creature that belonged there.

"A fine spot this is," Grandad said. "Good for thinking long thoughts. Did you have a grand time?"

"Yes!" Brian said. He was almost breathless with what he had learned, so Grandad spoke again.

"And so did I. A man should always enjoy his own company." Grandad smiled and pulled himself to his feet. "Now, let's be going home, remembering that there's no need to tell Nora that only one of us got to the castle."

"Grandad," Brian said, but he stopped. If he talked about what he had discovered, the little people would find out. He must keep his knowledge to himself.

Grandad didn't ask him what he had begun to say. His eyes sparkled as though he knew.

"Will there be moonlight tonight, Grandad?" Brian asked.

"We've had enough soft weather for a while. Soon we can count on a bright moon and a clear night," Grandad answered. "If it were tonight it wouldn't surprise me."

Brian took a long breath. Now he was sure that

Grandad knew what he would find, and that was why he had brought him to the castle this afternoon. But Grandad had also given him a warning. Brian wondered how he could possibly have enough courage to face a pooka and those other awful things. On the other hand, he had to prove Grandad was right.

Grandad set a careful pace as they walked down the shadow-dappled road toward home.

The place belonging to the little people had been found, and the time was near. Brian had a plan, but could he carry it out? What if he tried and it failed?

"Are you cold, lad?" Grandad said.

"No," Brian answered. It wasn't the chill air that had made him shiver.

CHAPTER SIX

As they walked into the kitchen door Aunt Nora shouted, "You just missed your parents, Brian! It was not more than a moment ago when I hung up the telephone!"

"Mom and Dad? Where were they?"

"Calling from Dublin, no doubt about it, because Nora's still using her long-distance voice," Grandad said.

Aunt Nora cleared her throat and smoothed the skirt of her apron. "In any case," she said in a normal tone, "they were sorry they couldn't talk to Brian, but sent him their love."

Brian was sorry, too. He missed his parents. There was so much he wanted to tell them. Even though he read over and over each post card and letter they had sent him, he had written very few letters to them. He really didn't like to write letters. It was too hard to put all the things he saw and felt into words.

65

He hung his jacket on one of the pegs by the door as Aunt Nora added, "They decided to skip the last series of lectures, so they'll be coming here for you the end of the week."

"Oh, no!" Brian said.

Aunt Nora and Grandad looked at him in surprise.

"I mean, that's just three days," Brian said. He looked at his great-grandfather, who began to settle himself into his kitchen chair as though arranging and rearranging each bone. He knew that this might be the last summer he'd ever have with Grandad, and much as he'd like to see his parents again, he didn't want to leave this man who was as wonderfully magical as the little people he knew so well.

"I'd like to stay here longer," Brian said.

"Well, now." Aunt Nora put an arm around his shoulder, giving it a gentle squeeze. "It's the fine boy you are, Brian. You'll not be the only one sorry your visit has come to an end." She added, "And it's welcome you'll be whenever you want to come back."

Brian didn't answer as he and Grandad looked at each other. Coming back would never be the same.

Aunt Nora was brisk and busy once more. "Wash up for supper," she said, and she began slapping the knives and forks on the table.

Brian splashed through the soap and water as fast as he could, because the bathroom was chilly. He hurried back to the warmth of the kitchen and the buttery fragrance of the roasting potatoes.

Uncle Martin pulled off his boots and coat as he came in the door, sidestepping Lady who hurried past Blossom to her feeding dish.

"Looks like a clear night," he said, and for a moment Brian held his breath. His parents were coming in only three days. If he were going to carry out his plan, he'd have to do it soon. Tonight? He glanced out the window, where the summer days stretched into long, lavender hours. Here in the kitchen pookas seemed far away, but out on the road it would be a different matter. Could he do it for Grandad? Brian didn't know.

Aunt Nora heaped his plate with thick chunks of the boiled beef, crusty potatoes and golden turnips, but Brian found he couldn't eat.

"Are you ill, lad?" Aunt Nora's eyes went from his plate to his face, and she clapped a hand on his forehead. "No temperature," she added.

"I'm fine," Brian said. "I'm just not hungry."

"No boy who is not hungry is fine," she said. "Let's tuck you in bed and see what a good night's rest will do for you."

So Brian soon found himself snug in the chill room, his feet drawing heat from the towel-wrapped water bottle as though his body were a straw. Tonight would be a good night to carry out under the plan, he kept telling himself; but he huddled under the mound of quilts, watching the room slide into deeper shades of darkness, before he fell asleep.

The next day was so filled with sun that Brian shed his jacket, hanging it on a post as he opened the gate for Lady and her sheep. Green shimmered with gold, and Uncle Martin said, "It will be good to have clear weather for a few days."

"No clouds tonight?" Brian said.

"Not likely," Uncle Martin answered; so Brian—checking to make sure that Blossom was nowhere in sight—thought of the hidden glen again. If he were to go right after supper, before it was dark—if . . . .

Lady ran down the hill after a stray ewe, and Brian ran with her, forgetting everything but the joy of the sunlit day.

Brian ate ravenously at the noon meal, and Aunt Nora's mouth turned up at the corners, as satisfied a look as the one he'd seen on Blossom's whiskered face. "I knew it was just a matter of a good night's rest," she said. "Brian's feeling fine now."

She picked up a large serving bowl in each hand and said to Grandad, "Where is it the two of you will be going this afternoon?"

Grandad straightened, as though he were trying to sit a few inches taller, and said, "Perhaps today Brian will want to explore for himself."

"Aha!" Aunt Nora said. "The walk was too much for you yesterday, wasn't it? Didn't I say it was too far for a man your age to go?"

"A man my age is made of many ages," Grandad

said. "A part of me may seem to be old on the outside, but there is a young man within me who will always refuse to be old."

Aunt Nora sniffed. "The young man and the old man had better go down for a nap," she said. She put the bowls on the counter, scraping their contents into a smaller container. "Brian might walk into town again, if he likes. It's a spool of white thread I'm needing."

"I'll get it for you," Brian said.

"That's a healthier thing to do, in any case, than listening to more of your grandad's foolish stories." She left the room, closing the door behind her to keep the warmth in the kitchen.

Sometimes, when Aunt Nora said things like that, Grandad seemed to shrink. Brian, wondering if it was his great-grandfather's hurt he was sharing, took Grandad's warm, papery hand and held it tightly.

"Grandad," he said, "there's going to be a moon tonight."

"Is there now?" Grandad said, and his eyes twinkled.

Brian smiled. From the corner of his eyes he saw Blossom curl upward, stretch and listen. He put a finger against his lips and winked.

Grandad winked back. Brian had made up his mind what he would do. Pookas or banshees or whatever would come at him didn't matter at this moment.

Aunt Nora returned, dropping some coins in Brian's

hand, repeating at least three times the kind of thread she wanted. "I'd better write it down," she said with a sigh. "It's for sure your mind is skittering about somewhere else."

Brian laughed. Aunt Nora would never guess where that somewhere else might be. He knew he'd be afraid, but that didn't matter, because tonight he was going to do what he had promised himself he would do. And that was all that counted.

CHAPTER
SEVEN

After supper that evening Aunt Nora turned on the television set as she always did. Brian helped with the dishes, his hands trembling in his eagerness to return to the castle and his fear of what he might meet on his way. Finally Aunt Nora hung up her apron and settled into one of the wooden kitchen chairs.

Brian quickly reached for his jacket, which Uncle Martin had brought from its deserted spot on the far gate. "I think I'll go for a walk," he said.

Blossom's golden eyes opened just a crack, and she stared at him.

Fat, juicy mice, Brian thought. Blossom squirmed, squeezed her eyes shut and tucked her nose under the tip of her tail.

"Be sure to come back before dark," Aunt Nora said automatically.

But Grandad added, "There's a clear sky, and the moon will be bright; so if Brian's a mite late, there's no matter."

Before anyone could say another word Brian hurried from the house. He ran to the road and strode up the hill and down into the tunnel of trees, not stopping to listen for the quiet sounds. He thought about Charlie and what he would say if he knew what Brian was doing. Would Charlie be as scared as Brian was? He gave a nervous laugh, and the sound in the stillness was so strange that he hurried all the faster.

As he came near the tree stump where Grandad had rested, he stopped, holding his breath. Someone was sitting there. It was a thin young woman who nodded at Brian.

"Good evening," Brian said politely, and he noticed that the hair that curled from under the woman's kerchief was ginger-colored! *Show no fear*, he remembered. Brian took a step forward, and another step, and another. Just in case this woman was one of the little people in human disguise, Brian immediately began to think about baseball games and Charlie and stealing bases and eating ice cream bars.

She kept her eyes on him as he passed. Brian walked without stopping until the road curved, and only then he dared to look back. Darkness was spilling into the glen, blotting up the shadows into a deep blue twilight. It was hard to see, but the stump seemed to be empty. The ginger-haired woman had gone.

Brian walked on until the castle suddenly loomed out of the evening's dim light like a warning hand.

Brian came to a stop. Now was the time to be very careful.

He heard nothing but a wild swan crying across the lake, and the slap of a heron's wings. He saw nothing but darkness being sucked into the small places between the leaves and branches and rocks around him. Taking one slow step at a time, he climbed into the castle, settled behind a broken rock wall, and waited. He didn't know why he was waiting, but he was sure the answer would come.

The night sounds settled into their pattern: the lake waters slapping the rocks, the tiny twigs breaking, the leaves falling, the night birds stirring; and Brian breathed with it, feeling secure, until the sound he had been waiting for reached his ears.

The tiny piping of what sounded like a flute rubbed crosswise with the night rhythm. Brian stretched his cramped legs and rubbed them, cautiously getting to his feet. The music was stronger now, and laughter wove its way through the notes like another tune. It was the strangest thing Brian had ever heard, and he followed the sound.

As he thought it would, it led him past the brambles to the holly hedge. The moon was bright, and its light and his groping fingers found the triangle of stones. Carefully, trying not to make a noise, Brian parted the holly bushes just enough so that he could look through.

There, in the circle just a few feet away, in an in-

between-world glow, was a laughing, chattering group of little people, dressed in both bright colors and drab, skirts flying, scarves waving, and boots stomping as they leaped and whirled to the music of a flute. And directly below him, sitting on a flat rock, was a leprechaun.

He was short and wiry, with his stocky legs crammed into heavy boots. Under his stained leather cobbler's apron his pants and smock were a dull gray green, but the pointed cap he wore was a surprisingly bright red. The small face that peered from under the cap was as wrinkled and gnarled as an old piece of tree bark. His lips, clamped tightly on a rough, evil-smelling pipe, turned downward in a scowl as he glared at the dancers.

Now was the time—now or never. Brian pushed apart the bushes, leaned over and grabbed the little man's arm.

The music stopped. The little people stared at Brian. Brian was frightened, but he kept a tight hold on the leprechaun.

"Let me go!" the small man shouted.

"No!" Brian said.

The leprechaun wiggled and twisted and dropped his pipe, but Brian held on.

"You must let me go!" he screeched.

"If you grant me a wish," Brian said. "I know the rules."

At this the leprechaun stood perfectly still. "Ah," he sighed, "another greedy person after my gold."

Some of the little people giggled. "You will never get it," a tiny, round woman said.

"I don't want it," Brian answered.

"You don't want gold?"

"No."

"But leprechauns don't grant other kinds of wishes," she told him.

"He can grant the one I'm going to ask," Brian said. And he told them about his great-grandfather who had always believed in them and kept on good terms with them, and how he had to help Grandad prove it all to Aunt Nora, who thought that talk about the little people was only foolishness.

When he had finished his explanation, the little woman turned to the leprechaun and nodded. "I think you should go with him."

"I don't care if anybody believes in me!" the little man grumbled.

"That's true," someone said with a snicker. "Nobody cares."

"I care," Brian said.

"Nobody cares what you care," the leprechaun said.

Brian spoke firmly. "This is what I'm going to do," he told them. "Since I am bigger and stronger than this leprechaun, I am going to pull him up through the holly hedge very carefully, because I don't want to hurt him. And I am going to hold his arm and walk with him all the way back to my great-grandfather's house and through the door and into the kitchen. And I will say, 'Aunt Nora, here's your leprechaun!' And after she takes a good look at him, I'll let him go and never bother any of you again."

"Do what you will," the tiny woman said, "but stop interrupting our party! On with the music!"

Brian gently pulled the leprechaun through the gap in the holly hedge. He set him on his feet, never letting go of his arm.

The small man grumbled and muttered, then suddenly got a crafty look on his face. "If you'll be kind enough to tie my bootlaces for me, we can be on our way."

"I'm afraid you'll have to walk with untied bootlaces," Brian said. "It would take two hands for me to tie them, and I know if I let go of you, you'd be gone."

He began to walk down the road toward his great-grandfather's house, and the leprechaun had to hurry to keep from stumbling. Brian noticed that the straggling bootlaces had magically tied themselves. He didn't outwit me that time, Brian thought. But he knew he'd have to be wary. They entered the grove of trees that almost cut out the moonlight. Brian could barely see the road.

"A pooka travels this road after dark," the leprechaun said. "Pookas can be very dangerous."

"That's what Grandad said," Brian answered. He hoped the leprechaun couldn't feel him tremble.

From far off he could hear a pounding that grew louder and louder, coming closer. It was the thunder of a horse's hooves. Brian stumbled to the side of the road and held his breath, terrified at what might happen.

Around the curve in the road galloped a huge black horse that was darker than the dark around it. Its mane flew like tattered banners. Its eyes glowed like devil fires. Brian clenched his teeth to keep them from chattering and stared at the ground.

"Wave your arms!" the leprechaun screamed. "It's the only way to scare off a pooka!"

But Brian gripped the little man more tightly, and he kept his eyes on the ground. The hoofbeats pounded in his ears, then magically faded away. Brian looked around, and he and the leprechaun were alone on the road.

"Grandad told me what to do," he said to the leprechaun.

"How much farther are you going to take me?" The leprechaun was so angry his trick hadn't worked that he kicked at a stone. "Ouch!" he yelled, hopping on one foot.

"I can carry you if you like," Brian said.

"A fine idea," the leprechaun said, his mouth turning up as though he were trying to smile. "Hold out your arms, and I'll jump right in."

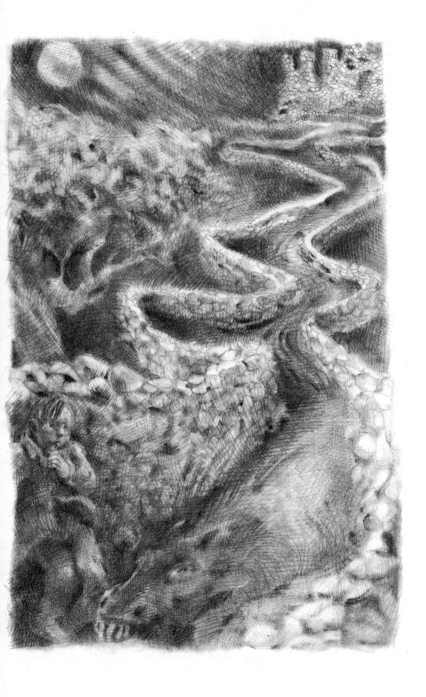

Brian didn't bother to answer. Without letting go of the little man's arm, he just tucked him up under his other arm and listened to him grumble as they climbed up the road that led over the hill.

"My great-grandfather's house is down there," Brian said. "We haven't far to go."

He was interrupted by a wail that seemed to come from over the valley, a crying, inhuman sound that made shivers crawl up his backbone.

"A banshee," the leprechaun whispered. "The only thing to do when you hear a banshee's cry is to hold your hands high in the form of a cross."

"Grandad says that the only thing to do is say a quick prayer," Brian said, and he did. The wail faded into the night.

He turned into the field next to the house. "I'm not asking much of you," he said to the leprechaun. "I just want Aunt Nora to see you. Then I'll let you go. You can hurry back to your party."

"I hate parties," the leprechaun said.

Brian knew that Grandad must have been watching from the window, because the kitchen door opened, and he came out on the stoop as Brian drew near.

"Ah!" he said in amazement. "Brian, lad, it's so surprised I am I don't know what to think!"

"Grandad," Brian said, "just seeing a leprechaun wasn't enough. I had to bring him here to prove to Aunt Nora that you're right."

The leprechaun grumbled, and Grandad quickly said, "A good evening to you, sir."

"It's not good," the leprechaun said.

"It's a grand thing you're doing, coming along with the lad to see his aunt Nora."

"I'm not coming along with the lad!" The leprechaun was so angry that he stammered. "If you'd take a good look, you'd see that he's carrying me where I don't want to go."

"He tried to trick me, Grandad," Brian said. "But I didn't let him."

"The tricks aren't over!" the leprechaun muttered.

Grandad studied the little man. "Did the boy ask for your gold?"

"No, he didn't."

"Then give him credit for that," Grandad said. "And I'm sure he might have something to give you for your trouble when this visit is over."

"Gold?"

"I don't have any gold," Brian said. "But I do have a bag of those chocolates that look like gold coins. Would you like those?"

"It happens that I did develop a taste for them," the leprechaun admitted. "So if you promise to leave the bag of those chocolates on the window sill of the barn tomorrow night, I might decide to forgive and forget."

"I'll do it," Brian said.

"Done," the leprechaun said. "Now if you'll be putting me down, I've got some paper and a pencil in my pocket. You can write out your promise."

"Later," Brian said, "after Aunt Nora has had a good look at you."

He carried the leprechaun into the kitchen and stood behind Aunt Nora's chair. Blossom's hair stood on end, and she crawled behind the stove. Lady rose with a low, protective growl.

"Brian," Aunt Nora said, not taking her eyes from the television set, "you missed a good comedy program. I thought you were going for a short walk, and here it is so late that your uncle Martin's already taken himself to bed."

"Aunt Nora, please turn around," Brian said. "I've got something to show you."

Aunt Nora turned slowly and looked at the leprechaun. She stared, and her eyes grew wide. Brian grinned at her.

"Brian!" she said, "where did you get that cat? It's the biggest one I've ever seen! I think that might belong on the O'Malley place. I've heard they have a very large cat."

"Cat?" Brian shouted. "Aunt Nora, this isn't a cat! It's a leprechaun! I caught him to bring to you to prove that Grandad is right!"

Aunt Nora pushed back her chair. "Brian, we'll have no more silliness about leprechauns and little people and the like. Anyone with two eyes can see that you're holding a very large cat. I think you should put it outside and let it go back to where it belongs. Stop trying to play foolish games with your aunt Nora."

The leprechaun began to laugh and shriek so hard that Brian could hardly hold him. "I could have told you she couldn't see me!" he shouted.

"Look, the poor cat wants to go home," she said. She took the leprechaun out of Brian's arms and stroked his head. "There you go, kitty," she said. She opened the back door and put the leprechaun on the stoop. He jumped up and down in glee and ran off as fast as he could go.

She turned to face Brian, putting her hands on her hips, and let out a sigh. But the corners of her mouth began to turn up, and the sigh became a gurgle as she tried to swallow a laugh. "Oh, Brian," she said. "You and Da are hopeless."

Then, stiff as her starched lace curtains, she added, "There's some berry pie left on the sideboard. I'm going off to bed, but you and Grandad can have some pie if you like."

Aunt Nora left the kitchen, and Brian turned to his great-grandfather. "I didn't know this would happen! The leprechaun tricked me and won!"

"He didn't trick you," Grandad said. He carried the pie pan to the table and cut two pieces, putting them on thick white plates.

"But he changed into a cat."

"No, he didn't. You and I saw him as a leprechaun. It was only Nora who saw a cat."

Brian dropped into the nearest chair and leaned his elbows on the table. "Why?" he asked.

"Because some people see what they want to see and hear what they want to hear. And that's the way the world is for them, and there's not much the rest of us can do about it."

"But you and I saw him."

Grandad raised his fork with a large, dripping piece of berry pie on it. "So I say, here's to us, and long may we see leprechauns and all the magical things that are there for the looking at."

"You don't mind that Aunt Nora still doesn't believe you?"

"Not a bit," Grandad said. "I think I'd mind more if she did see the leprechaun. She'd never stop talking about it."

Brian took a bite of the tart berries, wiping the juice from his mouth with the back of his hand.

"Tell me everything strange and wonderful that happened to you this night," Grandad said. "Not only do I want to hear every word, but it will give you good practice for when you're home again and telling it all to your friend Charlie."

"What if Charlie's like Aunt Nora? What if he doesn't believe me either?"

"Will that really matter?"

Brian thought a moment. Then he laughed. "No, it won't," he said. He took another large bite of pie, and he began to tell about the ginger-haired faerie and the banshee and the pooka and the fear and the darkness and the wonder of it all.

Grandad leaned toward him in his eagerness to listen, his eyes sparkling. Brian talked on and on, filled with the joyful bravery that follows fear, knowing this was the special moment, the time of magic that would belong to him forever.

C.1

NIX   Nixon, Joan Lowery

The gift

DATE			
APR 10 1985 NOV 0 2 1993			
MAY 3 1985			
OCT 2 9 1987			
DEC 18 1987 APR 2 0 1990			
MAR 4 1988			
	OCT 2		
	NOV 7		
FEB 0 2 1993			
MAY 0 4 1993 APR 1 7 1997			